Kitty's magic

Frost and Snowdrop the Stray Kittens

Bloomsbury Publishing, London, Oxford, New York, New Delhi and Sydney

First published in Great Britain in November 2017 by Bloomsbury Publishing Plc
50 Bedford Square, London WC1B 3DP

www.bloomsbury.com

A CIP catalogue record for this book is available from the British Library

ISBN 978 1 4088 8768 4

Typeset by RefineCatch Limited, Bungay, Suffolk
Printed and bound in Great Britain by CPI Group (UK) Ltd, Croydon CR0 4YY

1 3 5 7 9 10 8 6 4 2

Kitty's magic

Frost and Snowdrop the Stray Kittens

Ella Moonheart

BLOOMSBURY

LONDON OXFORD NEW YORK NEW DELHI SYDNEY

Chapter 1

'Well done, Misty!' whispered Kitty Kimura. 'You're behaving so well!'

It was December, and Kitty had come to the local vet's with her best friend, Jenny, and Jenny's mum. It was time for Jenny's silver tabby cat, Misty, to have a check-up.

Kitty had watched as the vet, Mr Singh, looked at Misty's eyes, ears and teeth, then gently picked up each of her paws to glance at her claws and the soft pink pads underneath. 'Everything looks fine,' he told Jenny's mum. 'It's very strange though. Most cats get so nervous about these check-ups, but Misty is very relaxed!'

Kitty hid a smile as Misty gave a pleased, proud purr. She knew why Misty was so relaxed. That morning, Kitty had explained exactly what would happen during her check-up, so Misty knew what to expect, and wouldn't be frightened. Kitty was really glad she'd been able to help. After all, Misty was her friend too — although that was a secret.

A few months ago, Kitty had learned that she had an amazing gift. She could

turn into a cat! The only other person who knew about this was Kitty's grandma, who had the same special talent. Kitty had found it very strange to begin with, but now she loved her exciting secret – especially as cats were her favourite animals in the world. Now Kitty loved nothing more than transforming into a cat while her parents were fast asleep at night, and exploring the village in her cat form – along with all her new cat friends, like Misty.

Kitty had even discovered that cats could speak to one another, just like people do. She also knew that cats could understand what people said, even though people couldn't understand a cat's miaows.

'Misty's such a good, brave cat!' said Jenny, lifting her carefully from the vet's table and cuddling her soft grey fur. 'Come on, let's get you home.'

It had been very chilly for the last few days, so the girls wrapped up warmly in their winter coats and gloves before they set off home. As they walked back to the street they lived on, with Jenny's mum behind them, something caught Kitty's eye. At the bottom of a fence were three small scratches in the shape of a triangle.

Someone's called a meeting of the Cat Council! Kitty thought excitedly. She glanced at Misty, curled in Jenny's arms, and saw that her ears had pricked up and her whiskers were twitching. Misty had obviously spotted the symbol too.

Whenever any cat in the neighbourhood had a problem, a question, or wanted to ask advice, they scratched the special triangle somewhere other cats would see it. Then everyone would come to a meeting of the Cat Council that night, in the woods close to Kitty's house.

I wonder who called this meeting? Kitty thought. *And I wonder what they want?*

That evening, while Kitty was eating dinner with her parents and grandma, her mum looked at her excitedly. 'Kitty, guess what? Your dad and I have finally found a new assistant for the shop!'

Kitty's parents owned a shop that sold special Japanese things. They were often very busy, and travelled to Japan a few times a year to buy new things to sell. They'd been looking for a new assistant to help them out for ages. Kitty didn't mind them going away though, because it meant she got to spend lots of time with her grandma, who lived with them.

'Her name is Nadia and she's going to start on Monday,' said Kitty's dad. 'We've invited her over for dinner soon, so you'll meet her then. She's very nice.'

'That's good,' said Kitty, nodding. But she wasn't really thinking about the shop. She was too curious about tonight's Cat Council meeting. Who could have called it? And why?

When dinner was finished and Kitty had helped clear the table, she gave a loud yawn. 'I'm really sleepy,' she said. 'I think I might go to bed.'

'But it's so early, Kitty,' said her mum, giving her a cuddle. 'You always used to love staying up late on Saturday nights, but you never seem to want to any more.'

'Yes, are you sure?' her dad said. 'Your mum and I thought we could all watch a film together tonight. You can choose it.'

Kitty hesitated. She loved film nights with her parents – especially as she and her dad liked acting out their favourite

scenes together afterwards. But she knew that she had to be at the Cat Council meeting tonight, no matter what. Grandma caught Kitty's eye and winked. She knew exactly why Kitty was keen to go to bed early. Kitty's grandma was able to turn into a cat too!

'I really am tired,' Kitty replied, pretending to yawn again and rubbing her eyes. 'I've had so much homework this week.'

'I could make popcorn,' her mum suggested. 'And hot chocolate with marshmallows. Your favourite!'

Those things did sound wonderful. Kitty's mouth watered at the thought of her mum's creamy, sweet hot chocolate. 'Would it be OK if we did it tomorrow?' she said.

'Goodness, Kitty, you must be really tired to pass up hot chocolate with marshmallows!' her mum exclaimed. 'OK, then, we'll do it tomorrow. Would you like me to come and tuck you in?'

'Oh no, I'm fine, honestly,' Kitty said quickly. 'Goodnight.'

After giving her parents and grandma a kiss, Kitty ran up the stairs to her bedroom and closed the door. Finally, it was time to get ready!

Chapter 2

As soon as she heard her parents going to bed, Kitty reached for the delicate silver necklace around her neck. The pendant had been a gift from Grandma. On it there was an engraving of a cat, above some tiny, mysterious words. Very quietly, Kitty said the words aloud:

> *'Human hands to kitten paws,*
> *Human fingers, kitten claws.'*

Straight away, a strange feeling whirled through Kitty's body. She closed her eyes, smiling as a ticklish sensation bubbled from the tips of her toes to the top of her head. When it faded away, Kitty opened her eyes and blinked a few times. Then she swished her tail and twitched her whiskers. She was a cat!

Kitty loved being able to jump and leap in her cat form. With a happy miaow, she sprang on to her bedside table, then on to the window sill. She slipped out of the open window and dropped on to the roof of the garden shed. A minute later she was trotting along her street, towards the woods.

When she reached the moonlit clearing where the Cat Council met, there was a group of cats waiting in a circle already. Everyone miaowed a greeting to Kitty when they saw her arrive, and one by one they ran towards her to gently bump foreheads. Kitty had learned that this was how cats say hello.

Misty was there, along with lots of Kitty's other friends, including an elegant blue-grey cat called Coco, a tiny ginger kitten named Ruby, and a slender, snowy-white cat with bright green eyes and a matching green collar, who was called Emerald. Kitty took her place next to Tiger, a big, bossy but friendly tom cat with black and ginger stripes, who always led the Cat Council meetings.

'Welcome, everyone!' he said. A small black cat with a delicate white patch on her head named Suki slipped into her place in the circle right at the last moment. Kitty purred happily when she saw the older cat arrive. Suki was a very special cat, especially to Kitty – because she was her grandma!

'Thank you all for coming,' Tiger said. 'Let's start by saying the Miaow Vow together.'

The cats chanted the special promise they all made at the beginning of every Cat Council meeting.

'We promise now,
This solemn vow,
To help somehow,
When you miaow.'

Tiger nodded approvingly. 'Before we begin, I wanted to give you all some important news,' he said. 'A fox has been spotted near the park. As you know, foxes can be dangerous, so please be careful!'

All around the circle, the cats nodded seriously.

'I was chased by a fox once,' said a tabby cat named Max, with a shiver. 'It was so big – and so fast! Luckily, some humans came past before it could hurt me and it ran away.'

'They have such sharp teeth. Even

sharper than a cat's,' added a Persian called Midnight. 'I'll definitely be keeping an eye out.'

'We should all keep watch — and please inform the Cat Council if you do see it,' said Tiger. 'Now, let's move on. Who called this meeting? Would the cat responsible please step forward?'

'It was me.' Emerald padded into the middle of the circle, her green collar glimmering in the moonlight. She hesitated for a moment, then looked round at the cats. Instead of sitting down, she stayed standing, with her legs slightly bent, as if she might run away at any second. Then she took a deep breath. 'I wanted to ask some advice,' she said.

'Advice about what?' asked Tiger.

Emerald paused. 'About ... about stray cats,' she answered finally. 'Like, if a stray cat came to our village, for example – what should they do? And where should they go?'

Kitty heard a slight tremble in her voice. Emerald looked so nervous.

Tiger turned to Kitty. 'As our Guardian, Kitty, would you like to answer?'

Kitty had a very special role in the Cat Council. She was the Guardian, which meant it was her job to try and solve problems for any cats who needed help. She took a step towards Emerald. 'Do you know of a stray cat in our village, Emerald?'

'No. No, I don't!' Emerald replied quickly, looking away. 'I was just curious, that's all. I don't know any strays around here. Not at all.'

Kitty thought this was rather a strange reason to have called a meeting of the Cat Council. Most cats who called a meeting had a serious problem that they needed help with. They didn't call a meeting because they were curious about something. Even so, she wanted to answer Emerald's question as best she could. 'Well, if a stray cat did come to our village, they should probably go to the cat rescue home,' she suggested. 'It's on the high street, next to the post office. I've heard that the humans who run it are lovely. And they make sure any strays who go there get a nice, cosy bed and lots of food to eat.'

'Kitty's right!' Coco piped up. 'And the humans at the rescue home help stray cats to find real homes too. They put pictures of the cat in the post-office window, and in the newspaper. Then any humans who want to give a cat a nice new home will know there's a cat who needs one. I've heard my human talking about it.'

Emerald frowned. 'But what if … I mean, surely rescue homes aren't the only places a stray cat can go to. Does anyone have any other ideas?' she asked, glancing round the circle.

'I agree with Kitty and Coco,' purred

Tiger. 'Rescue homes are the best place for stray cats to go. Very helpful, I hear.'

The other cats miaowed in agreement. Kitty watched as Emerald's tail and whiskers drooped. She thought she was acting really strangely, but she couldn't work out why. 'Emerald, why do you want to know this?' she asked carefully. 'Are you sure you don't need help in some way?'

'I told you, I was just curious. I don't need help. I don't need *any* help,' Emerald replied – but she sounded quite upset.

After Tiger had called the meeting to a close, Emerald slunk away.

Kitty quickly trotted after her.

'Emerald!' she called. 'Is everything OK? You seem – you seem a bit unhappy.'

Emerald tilted her head to one side, as if she was trying to decide what to say. 'You said that rescue homes are the best places for stray cats ... but I was a stray once,' she told Kitty, her voice a little shaky. 'When I was a kitten. I was taken to a rescue home by the people who found me. You're right that the humans there are kind, and they try hard to help you find a new home – that's how I met my human, Leo. But it's still a really scary place to be when you're tiny. There has to be a better place for stray kittens to go!'

And with that, she turned and ran away.

'Emerald, wait!' Kitty cried after her. 'Come back!'

But Emerald disappeared off into the woods.

Kitty sighed, feeling very puzzled. Something was definitely worrying

Emerald – but what? *I've got to find out,* Kitty thought to herself. *I'm the Guardian. If a cat is worrying about something, it's my job to help them.*

Chapter 3

'Kitty, catch!'

As Jenny threw a frisbee into the air, Kitty leapt to catch it, laughing. It was the next day, and Grandma had brought the girls to the park to play after school. Today was even colder, and there was a light covering of glittering frost on the grass, which crunched as they ran around on it.

Kitty turned to throw the frisbee back to Jenny and as she did, she caught a familiar glimpse of white slipping through the trees behind the swings. It was Emerald, glancing quickly from side to side as if she didn't want anyone to see her. Kitty spotted something small, shiny and purple held between her teeth. It looked like one of the pouches of tuna-flavoured cat food that Jenny fed to Misty.

Kitty had been wondering about Emerald's strange behaviour all day. Now it had got even stranger. Why was she bringing pouches of cat food to the park?! It seemed like a good opportunity to try and find out. Quickly, she flung the frisbee in the direction of the trees.

Jenny burst out laughing as the frisbee sailed out of sight. 'Kitty, that's miles away! I'd never be able to catch that!'

'Sorry!' replied Kitty, with a grin. 'I'll go and get it.'

She ran after the frisbee and ducked through the trees where she'd just seen Emerald. She came out into a small clearing, with a huge, old oak tree in the middle. It was surrounded by brambles and bushes. There was no sign of the cat anywhere – but as Kitty gazed around, she saw a few tufts of fluffy white fur caught in the brambles at the bottom of the tree. Emerald had definitely been there.

But why? Kitty wondered. And what had she been doing with the cat food?

Emerald lived on the other side of the village. Had she carried the food all the way from her house? And what, or who, was she carrying it for?

When Kitty went to bed that night, she lay awake, unable to sleep. The more she thought about Emerald's strange behaviour, the more she was certain that the white cat needed help. *She asked lots of questions about stray cats,* Kitty thought, remembering the Cat Council meeting. Emerald had said that she didn't know any strays around here – but what if she wasn't telling the truth? Kitty sat bolt upright in her bed. *If there is a stray cat in town, I've got to help!*

She glanced at the clock on her

bedroom wall. It was almost midnight. *That's it. I'm going to investigate — tonight!* she decided, throwing back the covers and jumping out of bed.

Kitty tiptoed into the hall to check that her parents were asleep. When she was sure she could hear their light snores, she crept downstairs in her pyjamas and out into the garden. It was a clear, crisp night with a bright full moon, and it was very cold. Her bare feet tingled on the frosty grass. Kitty shivered, thinking longingly about her warm, cosy bed upstairs. She shook her head. *If a cat's in trouble, sleeping can wait,* she told herself firmly. She clasped her necklace and muttered the mysterious magic words.

'Human hands to kitten paws,
  Human fingers, kitten claws.'

Kitty closed her eyes and waited. She grinned as the strange, magical sensation began whooshing through her fingers and toes, then up into her arms and legs. When it had passed, she opened her eyes and saw the trees and bushes of the garden through her much stronger cat eyes, all twinkling with a dusting of frost. Kitty was always amazed at how much better her cat eyes could see than her human eyes — especially in the dark.

Quickly, she leapt up on to the roof of her Wendy house, and from there she jumped on to the fence. She used her clever tail to keep balance, and trotted along it, past several neighbours' gardens, until she reached Jenny's house.

Misty was in the garden, batting a tennis ball around with her paws. 'Hi, Kitty!' she called when she saw her friend. 'I hoped you'd come and see me tonight. I wanted to talk to you about Emerald. I thought she was acting really strangely at the meeting last night. Didn't you?'

Kitty sprang down into the garden and ran over to Misty. 'That was exactly what I came to see you about!' she miaowed. 'I thought Emerald might have been hiding something last night. And guess what? I saw her again today and now I think she's definitely hiding something.'

Kitty explained what she'd seen in the park that afternoon. Misty listened, eyes wide.

'That sounds very mysterious!' she replied. 'I wonder what she was doing with the pouch of cat food?'

'Maybe we can find out!' Kitty suggested. 'Emerald lives on Willow

Street, near to my mum and dad's shop. I've noticed her there before, and I think I can remember which house she lives in. We could go there and try to talk to her.'

'Let's go now!' Misty purred eagerly.

Kitty followed Misty as she leapt through several flower beds, trotted round a vegetable patch, and ran down the road. The streets were quiet tonight because of the frost. Kitty knew that lots of her cat friends didn't like being cold. They would be curled up by a toasty radiator or fire tonight, or on a nice warm lap, instead of exploring outside.

The two cats scampered on to Willow Street, and Kitty pointed with a paw towards a small house with a blue door. 'I think that's Emerald's house,' she said. 'But we'd better make sure.'

Like the rest of the street, almost all the windows of the house were in darkness – apart from a dim golden light coming from a room on the ground floor. Kitty crouched down low then sprang up on to the garden wall. From there, standing as high as she could on her paws, she was able to peer in through the window. It looked into the kitchen, which was lit by a lamp on a small round table. Underneath the table, Kitty could see a cosy-looking, emerald-green cat bed, and a matching green water bowl next to it with EMERALD printed on the rim. 'It's definitely Emerald's house!' she hissed to Misty. 'All the cat things are green, just like her collar, and there's a bowl with her name on it.'

'Can you see Emerald?' asked Misty.

'No,' replied Kitty. 'Let's check the back garden – she might be out there.'

Kitty and Misty tiptoed down the path that separated Emerald's house from the neighbouring house, and into the back garden. 'Look, there's a bird table!' Misty exclaimed. 'Maybe we can jump up there and get a better look inside the house?'

But before Misty could try, Kitty's ears twitched. 'Wait a second. I hear something,' she whispered. 'It's a sort of creaking sound.'

Misty listened, and her eyes lit up. 'I can hear it too. It's coming from the front of the house,' she said. 'Kitty, I think I know what it is. The cat flap!'

'Quick – let's go and see!' miaowed Kitty quietly.

The cats rushed back down the path

and peered out from behind the side of the house. The cat flap in the blue door was swinging gently, and an elegant white cat was trotting away from the house and down the street.

'Look! It's Emerald!' hissed Misty. 'Where do you think she's going?'

Emerald's ears pricked up and she spun round, crouching low. She was holding something in her teeth. Kitty and Misty held their breath and didn't move. Everything was silent. Eventually, Emerald frowned, turned and carried on running down the road.

'Phew! That was close,' whispered Misty. 'She almost saw us. Did you see what she was carrying, Kitty? Another packet of cat food!'

'It's the same kind as before,' Kitty replied quietly. 'Come on, Misty – let's follow her.'

It didn't take long for them to realise where they were going.

'She's heading back to the park,' Kitty muttered. 'But why?'

They watched as Emerald trotted into the park, running past the playground and towards the trees. Kitty and Misty padded quietly after her. As they got closer, Kitty's ears pricked up at a sound.

'Listen!' she hissed to Misty. 'Do you hear that?'

Misty nodded. 'A miaow – a very faint one,' she replied.

'But it's not Emerald,' Kitty said. 'I

don't recognise who it is, but whoever it is sounds very frightened.'

She took another step towards the trees – and froze. All the fur on her body stood up on end, and without thinking, she crouched down low, her claws out, her paws ready to pounce and her tail swishing from side to side. Misty had done the same. A dark, shadowy shape with mean, glinting eyes had appeared by the climbing frame in the playground.

'Oh no, Kitty!' hissed Misty. 'It's a fox!'

'It must be the one Tiger warned us about last night,' breathed Kitty. 'If we stay really still and quiet, he might not notice.'

But to her horror, the fox sniffed the air, then turned its head – and the gleaming eyes looked right at them. Kitty gulped. She felt Misty trembling beside her.

'Well, well, well,' the fox said. 'What do we have here?'

'Quick, Misty!' squealed Kitty. 'Run!'

Chapter 4

Kitty and Misty dashed for the trees, running as quickly as their paws could carry them. They flung themselves into the clearing and crouched together, pressing their bodies down low. Even their ears lay flat. They waited for a minute, holding their breath. Finally, Kitty peered out bravely. The fox was loping away in the direction of the rubbish bins.

'That was close,' Kitty miaowed with relief. 'I think he's gone searching for some dinner in the rubbish bins, instead of chasing after us.'

'Phew!' sighed Misty. 'We were almost in real trouble then, Kitty!'

'Who's there?' hissed a voice nearby.

Kitty and Misty spun around. Emerald! They crept through the trees towards her voice, and Kitty caught sight of the elegant white cat. She was crouched in the clearing, next to the old oak tree where Kitty had spotted some tufts of her fur yesterday. She looked very anxious. Kitty took one more step forward, and a twig cracked sharply beneath her paw. Emerald jumped, arching her back and baring her teeth. Kitty had never seen her so alert before.

'Emerald, it's only us!' she miaowed, running into the clearing and towards the white cat. 'Kitty and Misty.'

'Hi, Emerald!' added Misty in her friendliest miaow. 'Don't worry. We saw a nasty-looking fox, but he's gone now.'

But Emerald didn't relax when she saw them. In fact, she arched her back even higher and took a few steps back. 'Stay away!' she hissed. 'Don't come any closer!'

'Why?' asked Kitty, puzzled. 'What's wrong?'

At that moment, she heard a noise: another frightened-sounding miaow.

'That's what we heard earlier!' said Misty, glancing around. 'What is it?'

'Is there another cat here, Emerald?' asked Kitty.

Kitty saw Emerald take a few careful steps to one side. *It looks like she's trying to hide something*, she thought. Quickly, she sprang forward and looked behind Emerald.

Kitty's eyes widened as she saw what Emerald had been trying to hide. Nestled in a hollow at the foot of the old oak tree, huddled tightly together and staring at her with nervous eyes, were two tiny, fluffy white kittens.

'I said stay away!' hissed Emerald again. 'I'm not going to let you take them to a rescue home, Kitty. I won't

let them be frightened there, like I was. I'm going to look after them myself.'

Kitty stared at Emerald. Suddenly, everything made sense. 'So in a way you were telling the truth at the Cat Council meeting,' she said. 'You didn't know a stray cat who needed help. You knew two stray kittens!'

'They're so cute!' purred Misty. 'I love their fluffy white fur. Where did you find them, Emerald?'

'I'll tell you if you both promise you won't make me take them to the rescue home,' Emerald said stubbornly.

'We promise,' agreed Kitty.

Misty nodded eagerly.

Emerald relaxed, lowering her tail and sitting down. 'They're called Frost and Snowdrop,' she explained. 'They're twin sisters and they're only two months old. They used to live in a different village, but their human moved house a few weeks ago. Frost and Snowdrop got frightened on the journey to their new home. They escaped from the car when their human wasn't looking. They hid in the park, and I found them here when I was out looking at the moon one night.'

'We were so scared,' squeaked Frost.

'And hungry!' Snowdrop yelped.

'Very hungry.' Frost nodded her silky head.

'I was so hungry my tummy started growling!' Snowdrop miaowed. 'But then Emerald saved us.'

'Yes.' Frost looked at Emerald gratefully. 'Thank you for bringing us food every night.'

Snowdrop sniffed sadly. 'It's getting so cold now, and our fur is so thin. I wish we could find our human again. She was really kind and gave us lovely cuddles.'

'The best cuddles,' Frost added.

'We shouldn't have run away from her,' Snowdrop said sadly. 'We'll never find out where she lives now.'

'We followed her scent to the park,' explained Frost. 'But then we lost the trail.'

Misty gave a sympathetic purr. 'Don't worry,' she said. 'Kitty is our Guardian, and she's really good at solving problems. She'll help you. Won't you, Kitty?'

They all looked hopefully at Kitty – even Emerald. Kitty took a deep breath. How could she help the kittens? How could she find the kittens' human in her big town?

'Do you know what your human's name is?' she asked.

The kittens shook their heads sadly.

'Never mind,' Kitty reassured them. 'Let's try something else. Do you think you could describe her?'

To Kitty's relief, both kittens nodded eagerly.

'Yes!' squeaked Frost. 'She's very, very tall.'

'That's a good start!' said Kitty.

'Anything else? What colour hair does she have?'

Snowdrop wrinkled her little nose. 'What's hair?' she asked.

'It's a bit like fur,' Kitty explained, trying not to smile. 'Humans have it on their heads.'

'Oh, our human has lots of hair!' replied Snowdrop excitedly. 'It's pink!'

Kitty was surprised. 'Pink! Are you sure?'

The kittens nodded.

'Oh yes,' Frost said. 'It's as pink as your nose.'

'Well, that definitely helps,' Kitty said. 'A very tall person with pink hair. There can't be too many of them around! I'm sure we'll find her really soon.'

The kittens miaowed happily, and Emerald purred.

'Where should we start?' she asked.

'I think we need to ask all our cat friends for help,' Kitty decided. 'We'll call a meeting of the Cat Council for tomorrow night. Emerald and Misty, please will you help me send out the message?'

'Sure, Kitty!' miaowed Misty, jumping up. She ran to the nearest tree and used a sharp claw to draw a triangle on the trunk.

Emerald looked wary again. 'What if the Cat Council decide we should take the kittens to the rescue home?' she asked.

Kitty placed a paw on Emerald's reassuringly. 'If we can find the kittens' human, they won't need to go to the rescue home,' she said. 'And thanks to the kittens' description, we *will* find their human. I'm sure of it!'

Chapter 5

Kitty couldn't get Frost and Snowdrop out of her mind all night – and they were the first thing she thought about the next morning when she woke up. *Will I be able to find their owner?* she wondered as she brushed her teeth and got dressed for school. *Will the Cat Council be able to help?* Kitty really hoped so.

At school, Kitty asked everyone in her class whether they knew a very tall woman with pink hair. She even asked the teachers, the librarian and the lolli-pop man who helped them cross the road outside school. But all of them shook their heads and said no. Some of them gave her a funny look too!

'My uncle's very tall, but he has grey hair. Does that help?' Kitty's friend Louis offered.

'No, it's definitely pink,' Kitty replied.

'I know a girl with bright pink hair!' said another of her friends, called Jack. 'She works in a cafe near my house.'

Kitty felt her heart jump. 'Really?'

'She's really small, though,' Jack said. 'So it can't be her, if you need someone tall.'

'Why are you asking anyway, Kitty?' Jenny wanted to know.

'Oh ... I, er, found a purse in the park. When I looked round, I saw a tall lady with pink hair walking away but she – er – jumped on a bus before I was able to give it back,' explained Kitty, thinking quickly. Luckily, Jenny and the others seemed to believe her.

Grandma was waiting to pick the girls up from school. Kitty suggested that they walk home through the park, hoping to catch another glimpse of the kittens on the way, but Grandma shook her head. 'We have a guest coming for dinner tonight,' she reminded Kitty. 'Nadia – the new assistant at Mum and Dad's shop. So we can't be late.'

For a moment, Kitty wondered if she should tell Grandma about the kittens. Surely Grandma would let her go to the park then! But Jenny was with them, and she'd overhear. Kitty knew she had to keep her magic secret from all humans, even Jenny. *I'll tell Grandma tonight at the Cat Council,* she decided.

When they arrived home, Kitty's mum and dad were carrying boxes from the garage and stacking them in the boot of their car. Kitty saw the markings on the boxes and knew they were full of Japanese trinkets, bought during her mum and dad's latest trip to Japan, ready to be taken to the shop tomorrow and sold. A small, very pretty lady with dark brown eyes and a silky headscarf was helping them.

'Kitty, this is Nadia!' said Mrs Kimura. 'Nadia, this is our daughter, Kitty.'

Nadia smiled at Kitty. 'It's so nice to meet you,' she said. 'Your mum and dad have told me all about you.' She

nodded at the necklace around Kitty's neck. 'Your necklace is so pretty. I like the little cat pendant. I'm a big fan of cats too.'

Kitty's dad clapped his hands together. 'That's the last box!' he said. 'Thanks for your help, Nadia. Now let's go inside and eat.'

Kitty's dad had made one of Kitty's favourite Japanese meals. As they ate, Kitty's parents, Nadia and Grandma talked about the shop. 'What do you think of the things we brought back from our latest trip to Japan, Nadia?' asked Kitty's mum.

'I love them,' Nadia replied with a smile. 'The silk parasols are beautiful. My favourite things, though, are the little smiling cat ornaments – the ones with their front paws raised up. They're so pretty.'

'Oh, those are called *maneki-neko*,' said Kitty's mum, sounding pleased. 'They're considered very lucky in Japan. Kitty loves them too, don't you, Kitty?'

Kitty nodded, but thinking of the little china cats made her mind drift back to the kittens. She couldn't wait for the Cat Council that night. She really hoped that the other cats would be able to help her find Frost and Snowdrop's human.

Later that evening, Kitty padded into the middle of the Cat Council and looked around at the circle of friendly, whiskered faces. She knew that Misty had been spreading the word about the meeting all day, telling every cat she met that the Council had an extra-serious problem to solve. It seemed as though every cat in town had come along to the meeting, eager to help out.

Grandma was at the meeting again

tonight, too – in her cat form, of course. She already knew why Kitty had called the meeting. Kitty had told her about the kittens on the way there. She was perched quietly between Tiger and Misty, and nodded encouragingly at Kitty. Emerald was there too, looking worried but hopeful.

'Thank you all for coming!' Kitty miaowed gratefully. 'The reason for this meeting is that Emerald has found two stray kittens in the park. They're very tiny, and they've lost their human. They need our help to find her again.'

A chorus of muttered miaows broke out around the circle.

'Oh dear, how awful. The poor little things,' Coco tutted sympathetically.

'And in this cold weather too,' Shadow added sadly.

'Kitty, have the kittens tried sniffing the pavements for their human's scent?' asked a cat named Buddy. 'That's what I did when I got lost once. I followed my nose all the way home!'

A few cats miaowed approvingly.

'Good idea!' called Tiger.

'They tried to do that,' Kitty explained. 'The trail led them to the park, and then they lost it. So they think their human must be somewhere close by. They just don't know where exactly.'

'Can the kittens tell us what their human looks like?' asked Tiger.

'Yes, she's a very tall lady with pink hair,' explained Kitty.

There was a murmur of surprise from the circle.

'What a funny description!' said Coco.

Kitty nodded. 'I know, but the kittens are certain that's what she looks like.'

'Perhaps we should all search a different area of the village,' suggested Ruby. 'We could peep into windows and look for a tall lady with pink hair. We could also keep an eye out for empty cat beds and bowls inside other houses. They might belong to the missing kittens.'

'That's a really clever idea, Ruby!' said Kitty. 'Does anyone have any other suggestions?'

'I'll go and look at the notices pinned up in the post-office window,' offered Coco. 'The kittens' human might have put a picture of them there. I wouldn't be able to read the human writing on the notice, of course – but you could, Kitty!'

Kitty nodded. 'Let's all get into teams,' she said. With her front paw, she drew a large rectangle in the ground, and then drew two crossed lines running across the middle of it. 'Imagine this is our village,' she said, and all the other cats gathered closer. 'Ruby, please will you lead one team, and search this area – the houses near to the railway station? Coco, you can take another team and look around this area – all the streets near the school and the village hall. Tiger, why don't you search this part, near the shops and the market? And, Shadow, this bit's yours – the houses close to the vet's.'

'Of course, Kitty,' Shadow replied. All the other cats miaowed eagerly.

'Let's go right away!' purred Ruby. 'We'll search all night if we have to, Kitty.'

'Remember – you're looking for a very tall lady with pink hair,' said Kitty. 'Good luck, everyone. Let's all meet back here tomorrow night to tell each other what we've found!'

After school the next day, Kitty wanted to run straight home so that she could go to bed early, and then secretly sneak out to search for the kittens' owner. But Jenny reminded her that they had plans. 'My mum's taking us Christmas shopping, remember?' she said excitedly, wrapping her scarf around her neck and pulling on a woolly hat.

Kitty felt disappointed for a moment, but then she realised she was in luck. *I can still search for the kittens' owner*, she thought. *I'll just be in my human form — and Jenny might even be able to help me.* 'Great!' she replied, smiling. 'I can look for that person I was telling you about. The lady whose purse I found!'

'Oh, yes! The tall lady with the pink hair.' Jenny nodded. 'I'll look out for her too, Kitty.'

The village high street was very busy, with lots of people shopping for Christmas presents. Golden, star-shaped lights twinkled overhead and some shops were even serving mince pies and hot chocolate to their customers. As Jenny's mum paid for some Christmas cards,

Kitty and Jenny stood outside the shop, nibbling on mince pies and looking at every person walking past.

'There are lots of very tall people,' Kitty said thoughtfully. 'But most of them are men, and we're looking for a woman. And no one has pink hair!'

'Only the girl who works in the cafe, like Jack said,' added Jenny. 'And he was right – she's really small, so that can't be who you saw. Maybe you should put an advert in the paper or something, Kitty? Or just take the purse to the police station.'

Just then, Kitty heard a warm miaow by her feet. She glanced down and grinned. It was Tiger, with Bella and Max – the team of cats searching this

part of town! She knelt down quickly, pretending to stroke Tiger's fur, and whispered, 'I haven't found anything yet, but I'll keep looking.' She knew the cats would understand her human speech, even though she couldn't understand their miaows.

Kitty did keep looking – right up

until the moment that Jenny and her mum dropped her off at her front door. But she didn't see anyone who matched the kittens' description. She just hoped that one of her cat friends would have found out something to point them in the right direction.

But when the Cat Council met again that evening, everyone seemed glum.

'We didn't see any tall, pink-haired humans at all. And there were no notices in the post-office window either,' sighed Coco.

'We looked in every house we could find,' added Ruby, with the rest of her team nodding in agreement. 'But we couldn't see any human who matched the description. And we didn't see any empty cat beds or water bowls either. I'm really sorry, Kitty.'

'Thanks for trying, everyone,' said Kitty, feeling disappointed. 'I guess we'll have to just keep looking.'

Grandma joined Kitty as the meeting ended, and they started trotting home together. 'Don't worry, Kitty,' Grandma reassured her. 'We'll find Frost and Snowdrop's owner soon. I'm sure of it. There can't be many people in the village with pink hair.'

Just then, Kitty felt a sting of something cold and damp on her fur. She looked up, and her heart stood still. It was starting to snow!

Usually, Kitty loved the wintry weather – but she knew that the cold was dangerous for the little kittens and snow would make matters even worse.

She looked at her grandma anxiously. 'Grandma, what shall we do? We can't let Frost and Snowdrop stay outside in the snow all night,' she said.

Emerald came running up behind them. 'We have to take them somewhere warmer,' she miaowed.

Grandma nodded seriously. 'I have an idea,' she answered. 'Quick – let's go to the park!'

The cats raced through the village as the snow began to settle on the ground. Once they were in the park, Grandma said, 'Now, Kitty – where are these kittens hiding?'

'Over there, behind that clump of

trees,' Kitty explained, pointing a paw. 'What's your idea, Grandma?'

'You'll see!' answered Grandma.

They began running towards the trees, but a sudden growl cut through the quiet of the empty park.

'Back again, little cats. And with a new friend this time?' it said.

Kitty spun around – and froze. 'Grandma – it's the fox!' she whispered.

The fox was watching them hungrily from the other side of the park. With a swish of its tail, it began padding towards them, its sharp teeth bared.

'Let's run!' Kitty hissed to Grandma and Emerald. 'We'll have to come back for the kittens tomorrow.'

But Grandma shook her head. 'No,

what if the fox finds them too? Let's scare him away, the horrible bully,' she whispered. 'Emerald, you keep back and, Kitty, when I say, change back into your human form. Ready? Steady? NOW.'

The fox was getting closer and closer, and Kitty felt her back arching and her tail begin to point right up, the way it always did when she was frightened. She heard Grandma softly whisper the mysterious, magical words to change back into a human, and somehow, very shakily, Kitty managed to say them herself. She closed her eyes as the fizzing whooshed through her paws, ears and the tips of her whiskers …

… and opened them again to see the fox backing away.

'What's going on?' he said in a frightened voice. 'One minute you had four legs and fur and now – now you've got two legs and you're human!'

'Yes, and that's not all we can do!' Kitty said bravely, taking a step towards him.

'Yikes!' the fox yelped, and he raced out of the park without a backward glance.

Kitty gave a deep sigh of relief. Beside her, Grandma was chuckling. 'He wasn't expecting that, was he?' she said, smiling. 'You were very brave then, Kitty – I'm so proud of you! Right, time to get those kittens. Now that we're both in our human forms we'll be able to carry them back home a lot more easily.'

Kitty stared at Grandma. 'Carry them back home?' she repeated. 'But ... but we can't take them home. Mum and Dad think I'm allergic to cats, remember? They'll never let two kittens inside the house!'

Grandma's eyes twinkled. 'Ah, but ours isn't the only house they can stay in. There's another one. Can you think what it is?'

Kitty frowned. 'Another house? You mean Jenny's house?'

Grandma shook her head. 'I'll give you a clue. It's very close to our own house — even closer than Jenny's. In fact, it's in the garden.'

Kitty's eyes lit up. 'I know! The Wendy house!'

Chapter 6

Kitty, Grandma and Emerald made their way over the snow-covered ground to the kittens' cold little nest in the clearing.

'Emerald, you'd better explain to them who we are,' Kitty said. 'They've never seen me in my human form before. We don't want to frighten them.'

As Emerald miaowed to the kittens their eyes grew wide with surprise.

'You're a cat who's able to turn into a human?' Frost yelped.

Kitty nodded.

'That's so cool!' Frost sighed.

'When we grow up will we be able to turn into humans too?' Snowdrop asked, looking excited.

'No, I'm afraid not,' Kitty said with a smile. 'Now let's get you somewhere nice and warm.'

With Emerald trotting along beside them, Kitty and Grandma carried Frost and Snowdrop from their nest back to their house, shivering as the snow fell even more heavily. While Grandma tiptoed into the house to fetch blankets for the cats to cuddle up in, Kitty rubbed them both gently with a towel until their white fur fluffed out like cotton wool. 'There, now you're both nice and dry, and hopefully a little bit warmer,' she whispered. 'You've got to stay hidden inside my Wendy house, OK? If my mum or dad see you, they might take you to the rescue home – and then we'll never find your real human.'

The kittens purred gratefully and rubbed their little heads against Kitty's hand. Kitty couldn't help smiling at them. They were so adorable. Surely their human wanted to find them, just as badly as they wanted to find her?

The next day Kitty got up extra early to sneak some food down to the Wendy house before breakfast.

'I'll come and check on you as soon as I get back from school,' she promised them.

But when she got home that afternoon Nadia was at Kitty's house for dinner again.

'Nadia has worked so hard in the shop today – we wanted to thank her,'

Kitty's mum explained as she handed out plates of spaghetti.

Kitty tried really hard not to frown. It was lovely to see Nadia again but now she wouldn't be able to check on the kittens for ages. She hoped they were OK.

'It looks delicious! Thank you,' said Nadia as she picked up her fork.

But Kitty couldn't help noticing that Nadia looked a little sad and tired.

Her mum seemed to notice it too. 'Is everything all right, Nadia?' she asked gently when Nadia let out a big yawn. 'I hope we haven't been working you too hard in the shop!'

'Oh, no! I'm really enjoying it,'

Nadia replied. 'I'm tired because I've been having trouble sleeping recently.'

Just then, Kitty caught a glimpse of movement out of the corner of her eye. She turned – and gasped. Two tiny, fluffy white heads were peeping through the patio door. Frost and Snowdrop!

If the grown-ups see the kittens, they'll take them straight to the rescue home. I promised Emerald I wouldn't let that happen, Kitty thought desperately. *I've got to distract them!*

'Er, does anyone want a glass of water?' she asked, jumping up from the table so that she blocked the door from view. Her parents and Nadia looked at her oddly. Kitty saw Grandma glance towards the patio door herself, and caught a look of worry on her face. She'd seen the kittens too – but how long until the others did?

'There's water on the table already, Kitty,' her dad pointed out.

'Oh. I mean – I might just grate some more cheese for the spaghetti,' said Kitty quickly.

Kitty's mum looked puzzled. 'Kitty, everyone's got plenty of cheese. I don't think we need more.'

'How about napkins?' Kitty offered desperately. 'We might all get spaghetti sauce round our mouths.'

'Well … I suppose that might be a good idea,' her mum said doubtfully.

'You are behaving a bit strangely, Kitty. Is everything all right?'

Behind her, Kitty heard a tiny, high-pitched squeak, and a gentle pattering sound. Her mum and dad frowned and Nadia's eyes opened wide.

'What was that sound?' she asked.

Kitty glanced around quickly. One of the kittens – Snowdrop – was batting her tiny paw against the glass of the patio door, and miaowing eagerly. Her sister had managed to climb up on to some plant pots and was about to jump on to the window sill. Kitty saw with horror that the window was slightly open, to let some fresh air into the warm kitchen. The kitten was about to come inside!

Maybe they're worried because I didn't come to see them after school, she thought. *But they're nice and warm and safe in the Wendy house. I told them they mustn't get seen by the grown-ups. Don't they know what will happen if they're spotted?*

The miaowing noise came again, and this time Nadia stood up. 'Can you hear that?' she asked. 'It sounds just like ...'

'I think it's a dog barking,' Kitty said quickly. 'Like this: Woof! Woof! Woof!' she yelped, trying to cover up any more noise from the kittens.

'Kitty, what on earth has got into you?' her mum said.

Her dad looked at Kitty and raised his eyebrows.

'Woof! Woof!' Kitty carried on. She

didn't care if she looked crazy. She couldn't let Nadia see the kittens.

But before Kitty could stop her, Nadia took a step towards the patio door. She peered around Kitty – and her mouth dropped open in surprise.

'Frost! Snowdrop!' she cried.

Kitty stared in astonishment as Nadia ran to the patio door and flung it open. She bent down and picked up Snowdrop, burying her face in the kitten's snowy fur. Then she crossed to the open window and scooped up Frost. Both kittens were purring so loudly that Kitty thought it sounded like a motorbike was driving past outside.

'Nadia, what's going on?' Kitty's mum asked. 'Whose are those kittens?'

Nadia burst into happy tears. 'They're mine!' she exclaimed.

'What?' cried Kitty. She looked at Nadia, cuddling the kittens, and her headscarf nestled up next to them. *Nadia's headscarf is pink!* she realised. *That's what the kittens meant by pink hair! And although Nadia isn't very tall to me, she must seem huge to Frost and Snowdrop. All this time we've been searching for someone tall, with pink hair — and really, the person we needed to find was small, with a pink headscarf!*

'Their names are Frost and Snowdrop,' Nadia explained happily. 'They're sisters. They managed to escape from my car when I was moving house. I didn't realise they'd gone until

I got to the new house and unpacked their travelling case. I've been so, so worried about them! I've searched all over the village. I thought I'd lost them forever.'

'But they were right here in our garden!' said Kitty's mum, shaking her head in amazement. 'I wonder how they got here?'

Grandma chuckled. 'It's like magic,' she said, winking at Kitty. 'Nadia, you are so lucky. They are the most beautiful kittens.'

Nadia beamed. 'I can't believe I've found them again,' she said.

Kitty reached out a hand and stroked the little kittens' fluffy heads. They both closed their eyes and purred noisily, and Kitty giggled. The kittens had found their human again – in the most unexpected way!

That night, Kitty, Grandma and Misty set off on a journey around the village. They wanted to tell all the other cats that Frost and Snowdrop's human had been found and the search was over at last!

Every cat they saw was delighted at the news – but when they reached the house with the blue front door, one cat seemed a little bit sad too. 'I'm so happy they've found their home, of course,' explained Emerald. 'But I have to admit, I loved seeing Frost and Snowdrop every night, and looking after them. I'm going to miss them very much.'

'No, you won't!' squeaked a tiny voice.

Kitty purred happily as Frost and Snowdrop scampered up to them. Their fur had been neatly combed and they were both wearing smart new collars, with their names engraved on silver pendants. 'What are you doing here? It's very late – you kittens should be fast asleep!' scolded Emerald, but Kitty could tell the white cat was secretly very pleased to see them.

'As soon as Nadia went to sleep, we decided to come and find you!' Frost explained.

'We've made sure we know how to get home again, though,' added Snowdrop. 'We don't want to get lost for a second time.'

'But it turns out we live just round the corner!' miaowed Frost happily. 'We've got a lovely, cosy bed each, lots of toys, and best of all, a cat flap in the back door. So we can come and visit you every night, Emerald.'

'And you too, Kitty!' miaowed Snowdrop shyly.

'I'd love that!' replied Kitty. She was so pleased the kittens had found their new home – and had made so many friends already. She wondered what her next cat adventure would be!

Kitty's best friend has
a brand new kitten!

But Misty is too
scared to go outside.

Can Kitty use her magic and
help Misty to be braver?

Turn over to read some of
Kitty's first ever adventure…

Kitty's magic

Misty the Scared Kitten

Chapter 1

'Grandma! Grandma!' shouted Kitty Kimura excitedly. 'A postcard's arrived from Mum and Dad!'

Kitty ran to the kitchen. Emails were nice, but she loved getting post! The card had a picture of a waving ceramic cat on it. In Japan, they were a sign of good luck. Her parents were in Japan again now.

Grandma was pouring tea into her

flowery cup. She smiled as Kitty read the short message aloud and then stuck the postcard on the fridge.

Kitty's grandma had been born in Japan, but moved to England when Kitty's dad was little. Kitty's parents now owned a shop that sold special Japanese things, and Kitty loved all the silky kimonos, colourful fans and sparkly mobile phone charms. Three times a year, her parents went to Tokyo to look for new things for the shop.

Grandma lived with Kitty and her parents, so they spent lots of time together, especially when Mum and Dad were away. Kitty missed them, but she loved being with Grandma. They even looked alike, with the same almond-shaped eyes. But Kitty's hair was long and black, while Grandma's bob had a streak of pure white on one side of her fringe.

'What shall we do for the rest of the week, Kitty-cat?' Grandma said.

Kitty's real name was Koemi, but she loved cats so much that she was given the nickname Kitty, and now everyone called her that!

Just as Kitty was about to answer, the phone rang.

'I'll get it,' Kitty offered, running into the living room.

She picked up the phone. 'Hello?'

'Kitty!' said an eager voice. 'It's me, Jenny!'

Kitty was surprised. Jenny was her

best friend, but they hardly ever phoned each other, because Jenny only lived three houses away. 'Hi!' she replied.

'Can you come to my house for a sleep-over tonight?' Jenny burst out. 'I have something really exciting to show you!'

Kitty giggled. Jenny was always

cheerful, but today she sounded even happier than usual. 'What is it?' she asked.

Jenny paused for a second. 'Well … I was going to keep it a surprise until you got here, but I can't wait. I've got a kitten!'

Kitty gasped. 'Jenny, you're so lucky!' she said, a smile spreading over her face. 'Why didn't you tell me before?'

'I didn't know until today!' Jenny explained. Kitty could hear her friend bouncing up and down excitedly. 'Mum kept it a surprise until I got home from school. My Auntie Megan is moving to America and she couldn't take her kitten with her – so she's given Misty to me! Wait till you see her, Kitty. She's gorgeous. She's pale grey with darker grey stripes. Mum says she's a silver tabby. And I think she likes me already. As soon as Auntie Megan brought her over, she ran straight up to me and rubbed herself all around my ankles!'

'I can't believe it,' Kitty said wistfully. 'I *love* cats.'

'I know! That's why I rang you straight away,' Jenny replied. 'It'll be as if she's your cat too! So can you come? We can play with Misty all evening!'

'Let me ask Grandma,' Kitty told her friend. 'I'll call you right back!'

She put down the phone and raced back into the kitchen. 'Grandma!' she called breathlessly. 'Can I sleep over at Jenny's house tonight? She's just got a *kitten*!'

Grandma put down her teacup. 'A kitten?' she replied slowly. 'Well, that's lovely for Jenny … but, Kitty, you know you start to sneeze as soon as you're anywhere near a cat.'

Kitty bit her lip. It was true. Ever since she was a baby she had been allergic to cats. It made her feel sad and a bit cross, because cats were her favourite animals in the whole world. She loved their bright eyes, their silky fur, and the soft rumble of their purring.

Most of all, she liked imagining what the cats in her village got up to at night, when people were fast asleep! What made it even harder was that cats seemed to really like *her*, too. They always followed her down the street,

rubbing their soft heads against her ankles and miaowing eagerly. Kitty couldn't resist bending down to stroke them, but she always ended up with sore eyes and a runny nose.

'Oh, please, Grandma,' she begged. 'I'll take lots of tissues, and if I start to get itchy eyes or a tickly nose, I'll stop playing with Misty straight away, I promise.'

Grandma gazed thoughtfully at Kitty. 'Well, maybe you are old enough now,' she murmured softly, with the hint of a smile on her lips.

'What do you mean, Grandma?' asked Kitty, frowning. *Old enough that my allergy will be gone?* she thought, confused.

'Never mind,' Grandma told her, shaking her head. 'Wait here, sweetheart. I have something for you.'

Kitty bit her lip, curious. Grandma sometimes acted a bit strangely. She often took long naps at funny times, and she would stay up late, saying she was watching her favourite TV programmes. But now she was behaving even more oddly than normal.

When Grandma came back, she placed something carefully into Kitty's hands. It was a slim silver chain with a small charm hanging from it. At first Kitty thought there were Japanese symbols on it. But as she looked more closely, she saw it was a tiny picture of a cat.

'Wow,' breathed Kitty, slipping the necklace over her head. 'It's beautiful.'

Grandma smiled and reached under her blue silk scarf to show Kitty a matching necklace. 'I have one too,' she explained. 'They have been in our family for a long time. Yours belonged to your great-grandmother. I've been keeping it safe until the right moment. It's very precious, and I know you will take good care of it. Make sure you wear it at Jenny's house. I think it will help with your allergies.'

'You mean … I'm allowed to go?' cried Kitty. 'Thank you, Grandma!'

Kitty flung her arms around Grandma, though she was puzzled about what she'd said about the necklace. How

could a piece of jewellery stop her from
sneezing? But she was too excited to ask
questions. She was going for a sleepover
at her best friend's house, and she was
going to play with a sweet little kitten!

Chapter 2

Half an hour later, Kitty and Grandma set off for Jenny's house, swinging Kitty's overnight bag between them. As soon as Kitty pressed the doorbell, the door burst open. Jenny's freckled face was flushed pink with excitement. 'I couldn't wait for you to get here!' she said with a grin. 'Quick – come and meet Misty!'

Jenny led them into the kitchen, where Jenny's mum and little brother Barney were painting. Jenny's mum washed her hands and made a cup of tea for Grandma. Kitty looked around eagerly for Misty. 'Where is she?'

'Over there, on the window sill!' said Jenny.

Kitty gasped as she spotted the little cat. 'Oh, she's *so cute*!' she cried.

Misty was curled cosily in a beam of warm sunshine. She was a soft grey colour, with darker grey stripes all over her body, and long silver whiskers. Her eyes were a pretty blue. When she spotted the girls, she sat straight up with pricked ears and gave a happy mew.

FELINE FACTS

Here are some
fun facts about our
purrrfect animal friends
that you might like
to know ...

1.

The heaviest ever
domestic cat weighed
over **21 kilograms**!

2.

A kitten's **purring**
keeps it healthy

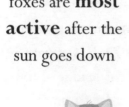

3.

All kittens are born with **blue** eyes

4.

Just like cats, foxes are **most active** after the sun goes down

5.

A cat named Stubbs has been **mayor** of a town in Alaska for nearly **20 years**

 # MEET

Kitty

Kitty is a little girl who can magically turn into a cat! She is the Guardian of the Cat Council

Tiger

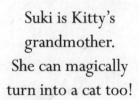

Tiger is a big, brave tabby tom-cat. He is leader of the Cat Council

Suki is Kitty's grandmother. She can magically turn into a cat too!

Suki

THE CATS

Snowdrop

Snowdrop is a
little kitten with
an amazing
sense of smell

Frost

Frost is Snowdrop's
twin sister. Frost's
favourite food
is tuna!

Emerald

Emerald is a very
fancy white cat with
green eyes. Emerald
has a big heart